Anna's Garden

Written and Illustrated by Sarah Hewitt

For my fairy goddaughter Sophia,

for Little Sarah,

and for all children everywhere.

Do what makes you happy!

TINY TREE

First Published in 2024 by
Tiny Tree Books

www.tinytreebooks.com

ISBN: 978-1-837914-84-5

Text and illustrations copyright © 2024 Sarah Hewitt
The moral rights of the author(s) have been asserted.

Apart from any fair dealing for the purpose of research, or private study, or criticism or review as permitted under the Copyright, Designs and Patents Act, 1988, this publication may only be reproduced, stored or transmitted in any form, or by any means, with the prior permission of the publisher, or in the case of reprographic reproduction, in accordance with the terms of licenses issued by the Copyright Licensing Agency. Enquiries concerning reproduction outside those terms should be sent to the publisher.

"What's your name?" says the girl with the beautiful hair.

"It's Anna," says Anna, "and I live over there."

"Do you want to play? I'll throw you my ball!"

"No thanks," replies Anna, "I won't like that at all."

"But thank you for asking, here's a present from me;
flowers will grow so pretty, you'll see."

"What's your name?" says the cat,
with a superior air.
"It's Anna," says Anna,
"and I live over there."

"Let's climb high," says the cat, "we can leap from the trees,
we can balance on branches, catch birds and chase bees!"
"No way," replies Anna, "I'm not having that!
I don't like to climb, not today Mr Cat."

"But here is a present and when it's in bloom,
come back and see me one day very soon."

"What's your name?" says the boy with the magical chair.
"It's Anna," says Anna, "and I live over there."
"Can I come and play? Let's blow up balloons;
let's huff and let's puff, until they go BOOM!"

"No thanks," replies Anna, "that's not nice at all!
But here is a gift, it will grow very tall."

"What's your name?" says a voice, and up jumps the hare.

"It's Anna," says Anna, "and I live over there."

"Come, hop in the field, and jump with me too!"

"Not likely," says Anna, "it's not what I do!"

"But here is a gift: look after it please,
and don't sniff the flowers, they might make you SNEEZE!"

"What's your name?" says a voice; it's the cuddly bear.
"It's Anna," says Anna, "and I live over there."
"Can I come to your house; do you want to play?
I'm feeling sad and I'm lonely today."

"Here's a big hug and a present for you.
Sit down beside me, here's what to do:
be gentle, be kindly and water each day,
look after my present and sad goes away."

"What's your name?" says the dog, with his tail in the air.

"It's Anna," says Anna, "and I live over there."

"Let's run up the hill and all the way down."

"No thanks!" replies Anna, with her face in a frown.

"But I'll give you a present to show you I care,

then call on the girl with the beautiful hair,

and go back to the cat with his nose in the air,
and look for the boy with the magical chair,
and please don't forget the hop-along hare,
and last but not least the cuddly bear!

Then when you have found them, bring all of them here;
tell them to bring back the flowers so dear."

Now lo and behold, a garden so bright!
A garden of friendship to welcome, delight.
All is so calm - not a leap nor a hop,
not a skip nor a jump, no balloons going POP!

Just bright happy flowers grown with love and with care.

"Welcome," says Anna, "here's my garden to share."